Tri With Mom

by Rachel Brenke

To all moms who tri
-Wherever you go, there you are.

I watch her get up early or stay up late.

She often has to break up her workouts to take us to school, or is unwrapping snack wrappers for us while she rides.

On race day, she gets prepared to swim, bike, and run to the finish line.

Where I will be waiting!

During her race, I love to hold up signs and ring a cowbell while yelling, "go mommy!"

She swims in big oceans and rivers where there are lots of creepy things in the water.

This doesn't bother her
because she is brave.

She rides her bike in strong winds and up big mountains.

She does it all with a smile because she's strong.

Even when she's already done
swimming and biking, she doesn't stop.

She keeps running and gives
me a thumbs up.

When she crosses the finish line, she raises her arms tall and smiles big because she just did something awesome.

After she gets her medal, she comes and gives me a big hug.

While she's stinky and sweaty, I love hugging her because I am so proud.

GO THE
DISTANCE

TRI

ATH

LON

I'm so proud of my mom.

Watching her be awesome makes
me think, I could do this too.

I get my bike out of the garage, strap on my helmet, and go for a ride.

When we go to the pool, instead of
diving for toys like everyone else,
I try to swim laps to get strong like mom.

I asked mom if I could run with her.
She smiled so big and we went for
a run together.

We even brought our dog along.

On race day, we loaded up my bike and got it ready in transition.

I was ready to be strong like mom.

I tri because my mom does.
I tri because she believes I can.

I tri.

Made in the
USA
Monee, IL